I Woke up on
The Wrong Side of Love

Sharita Renee

I woke up in love this morning, and I went to sleep in love. It was so routine. Until one day it no longer was, and I woke up on the wrong side of love. Where stomach butterflies turned into nausea. Once blue skies were now stormy and gray. This book is like a two sided coin. Love can also be that way. What side of love do you want to visit? Two sections of amazing poetry that allow you to visit both sides of this poets loving bed. Be prepared for laughter, smiles and tear-jerkers. Mental stimulation served to you poetically.

This book is dedicated to love.
Whether it was the highs of love or the very lows.
The love that appeared to be real but flipped to fake.
Love that makes you protect someone that lacks in protecting you.
Pure love that makes you wanna tell the world. Love that makes you wanna hide truths.
This book is so beautifully dedicated to the ones who know how to love and the ones still trying to figure love out.
Above all things this book is dedicated to you.

Peace and blessings to all,
~Sharita Renee

Table of Contents

Bottled up the Moments

Living in the moment
because every moment with you I'm living
Ever since I met you I wanted to nourish and never neglect you
See you must be my soulmate
I spoke to the Most High about you
Flabbergasted now
due to not recognizing love at the first sight of you
Forgive me baby
For I have been let down a time or few
by beings that resemble the tone of you

So glad I didn't give up on love
So joyful that I fell but got back up
Lover, love knocked me down,
hit me with a TKO
You came my way and I swear it was like,
I had never been knocked the fuck out by love before

You give me butterflies of the strangest kind
Maybe it's only strange because I'm finally getting what I give
You're so busy but make time for me
King, you never skip a beat
I was use to men that said they love me
but couldn't make time for me
I found that so ironic
The excuses they'd make would be iconic

I never missed birthday's
however that last guy missed all of mine
Now you have came along
and March 31st is marked on your calendar
Surrounded by hearts so glad I found ya
Dang, how did I get so blessed?

You came to me when I needed peace
but was too stressed
How you took your time to learn my heart
and investigate my mind
The last one had my heart,
I was ecstatic to have gotten it back
I give it to you with no strings attached,
Just don't break it
You might be average to the world,
to me you're one of a kind
It's the simple things you do
I'm lying..
it's just you

Spell On You

I put a spell on you and now you're mine
It wasn't spaghetti with menstrual surprise sauce
No voodoo that would later give you hair loss
See, I put a spell on you with my actions,
    that so elegantly reflected my words
Sexy black nerd and I heard I wasn't your type
Didn't shoot my shot not even in my sights
I can't read minds
but I knew what you were thinking

Nothing like most women you stick your thang in
Yet, I'm no saint without sin
Come and take a walk on my wild side
Allow me to put something delicious on your taste buds
and stimulate your mind at the same damn time

You are my Popeye
but I'm not your olive oil baby
I'm your spinach
You'll be weak without me,
    come and get your strength
Good for your body and mind, get use to it
If I was a blunt I'd be your first and last hit
It doesn't make sense how one look turned into a hug,
Hug into a kiss
Kiss into some love

You didn't even have to bite into my juicy apple to get hooked
I scaled your heart's walls like a crook
but I'm no thief
Didn't have to pick hairs out of your brush
Come to think of it, that would have been tough
I put a spell on you and it took some time
Manifesting that you'd be all mine
I didn't say I wanted a boyfriend

no, no, husband sounds so much better
Told the Most High I was ready to receive my forever
So I spoke it
I prayed and I hoped it
I put a spell on you because I merely spoke it

I didn't know what you'd look like,
I just set back and
Let the Most High handle that
Worked on myself and got my happiness back
Didn't want old heartbreak to hold me back
So speak it, write it down and believe it
Being in real love,
you can achieve it
but be ready to receive it
I shared my spell with you

Sorry it didn't involve scarifies pills,
potions nor voodoo
Love yourself first
Then watch the Most High do the Soul-searching for you
Nightmares are now beautiful dreams
Because now days I fall asleep
and wake up next to my king

Not Incomplete

I'm already whole
You should want me, not need me
See I've been the lighthouse for lonely ships with battered sails
I'm whole! One hundred percent
So I'm going to pour into you
and all you need to do is pour back into me
My cup isn't empty, it's full to the rim
I don't need a relationship built off financial gain
I don't need you to invest in a co-partnership with me
Be a name on my LLC
Make my Cashapp sing

Those aren't needs for me but if you want to
I'm not broken so I'm not giving up pussy
to a cat that don't wanna be in this house,
wearing his husband hat
See she needs you because she isn't a whole pie
she is only half

I want you because I am whole
You should want me because of that very thing
I'm the one that wants the love,
fuck the size of the ring
Thousands on a wedding?
Nope let's invest that into business
I'd marry you in a backyard

It was real love from the start

I Gave My Heart To You

I don't know if it's possible,
to be in love with two people at the same time
However, I know it's possible to be in love with somebody
and it never seems like the right time
So instead of putting in more and more time
I allowed somebody else to love me
In hopes that I can love him back
I already have his back
but I need to get my heart back from another
He is a good man in the outside world
but horrible at being a lover
This other guy loves out loud
he is proud to say I'm his
How can I be all in when my heart is with someone else?
Not even deserving of something so precious
He is my life lesson
A pain in my ass, yet I love him
I freeze up even at the thought of giving myself to another man
For four years there has been no other man
I remember when he use to send me poems
Damn I so badly want his words to reflect his actions

See he lives life in the fast lane
and I'm just a distraction

Just Stay

If I knew this time would be the last time I'd hear your laugh
I would have told more jokes
Smelling your scent on your coat helps me cope
I'd lose my mind today if that scent faded away
Closing my eyes longer randomly
just so I can see your face, isn't enough for me
Why'd you have to go away?
Nobody can say anything to ease my pain
It wasn't your time
That wasn't God's will nor mine
The Most High doesn't pull tiggers
I'm so mad at you right now
Damn! I miss you
Baby why couldn't you have just stayed home?
Not a street dude but the streets you roamed
I asked you to just stay home!

Tonight be here with me, I wasn't trying to fuss
You chasing the bag to make it better for us
All legit 'cause he was just that tough
I'm sleeping in your T-shirts cause I need you near me
Looking for clothes you had on last week,
that have yet made it to the laundry

I'm going crazy, must be crazy
I swear I heard you calling my name
Sug, I'm running around this house looking for you
Keep calling my name I'm going to find you
Your loud baritone is now a whisper,
I wimper
Tear drops are falling
The phone no longer rings
because everyone has stopped calling

16

Why didn't you stay?
You said you'd be home by 1:00 a.m.
Your usual time
Kissed me on my lips then released
I just stared at you
You must have felt it, 'cause
you turned around and pressed your lips against mine one more time
Wishing now I could turn back the hands of time
When I said I love you,
who knew that be the last time you'd say "I love you too."
Forgive me God I'm just confused
Why did my soulmate have to go
We had a lifetime more to go
Now time is moving just as slow,
as that night I waited up!

Texting you to see how it was going
"Baby my new bartender keeping the liquor flowing."
You told me to keep your side of the bed warm
Never did you warn me that I'd have to keep it warm forevermore

2:00 a.m.
you still haven't walked through that door
3:00 a.m.
you're not answering your phone
I left you a voicemail,
"Boy get yo' ass home, before I put my shoes on."
4:00 a.m.
I know something is damn sure wrong
Why is your brother calling my phone
Nope you bet not be drunk,
I'm not picking you up
I'm not going to keep putting up with the nightlife shenanigans
Laughing in my head because that must be what's happening

I answered the phone
he couldn't get his words out
now I'm panicking
He finally said *"sis they killed him."*
He didn't even have to say your name

17

I could feel this unfamiliar pain
I just screamed your name
Hoping you could hear me
That shooter didn't know,
but that night he took two lives
Baby why did you go?
Physically I'm here yet mentally I'm gone
That night I just wish you would of stayed home
Baby why did you go?
I will wait a life time for that answer
knowing I will never know
I don't know what I'll do with your scent is no longer present
Please don't go

Heaven Sent

My mother always told me
"you never know when you're entertaining an angel"
I thought that beautiful being with halos only dwelled in heaven
That's until I laid eyes on you
I had to check your back
No wings, but you're perfect
I hear 90s R&B in my head when you bless the room
Some *Jagged Edge* followed by *112*
Throw that *Slick* on we can't go wrong
Do you believe in love?
Because I believe you were sent from above
See you make a man want to love you for a lifetime
Yet I might need a couple of forevers
I just wanna vibe with you
Top down, loud sounds, I just wanna ride with you
Buckle your seatbelt love, lets go
To that place only lovers go
Body to body, as lips touch
I make you hit high notes
We can go with the flow that's up to you
Beautiful is an understatement when I'm describing you
Can I be the Sun that sets in your sky?
Can my rocket explore your Milky Way?
I would call you a star
but a Super Nova is more befitting,
so explode on me
Life gets hard lighting up your load on me

You're an angel without wings,
now I know what heaven on earth truly means

From a King to his Queen

Playing For Your Heart

I live my life above the rim
So much so
That my first real relationship was with *Spalding*
The only ball I was holding as life start unfolding
Magic Johnson
The only man on my brain
I can recall his stats from every game
Then you became the boy next door
It was a love at first sight
But back then I had selective hearing and sight
Yet my jump shot was mad tight
You left your permanent mark on me Quincy
As I rub my scar
Sitting back wondering where you are
You double dribbled my heart
I'm a ball player too Q!
The same as you; I never made you choose
When dogging me out became your practice
Running bitches yo' new position
Treating me like,
I was the sticky shit on the bottom of your game shoes

My ass, you taxed it
My love, you had it
But I wasn't missing practice
So when we good we good
When we ain't we ain't
You hit me with a pump fake
Crossed me over like A1
I can't even pretend that my heart you didn't win, back then
However as time progressed I still lone for you
I'm willing to lace up and take you to the hole if I have to
It's love and basketball
I'm ready to play the biggest game of my life

The grand prize? Your heart
The title, your wife
I can't keep living life without you
My Q man, I never doubted you
That one sided relationship just wouldn't do
Old girl might be cool
But you and me are meant to be
I'm ready to trade the Wright for McCall,
winner take all
Just pass me the damn ball

(Inspired by the movie "Love and Basketball")

Short But Sweet

I just need a few forevers with him
His eyes have always felt so familiar to me
Must have ran through the tall grasses together
Made sweet love under the moon top dropped listening to radio tunes

I have been with him before

Wish Upon A Star

Your heartbeat plays a melody that only I can hear
In your arms I relinquish my fears
Tears of joy when we finally let love win
I don't have the fattest ass
Nor the prettiest face
I was hoping that the goofy girl
that dances randomly was your taste
The type of woman that makes you a home
and supports your dreams
A Nubian Queen

You played a lot of games,
said a lot of things with no follow through
Yet for some reason I just couldn't be through with you
I want you baby I truly do
However you need to play by my rules
Consistency is sexy
Showing me love and respect is necessary
No negotiation, love me correctly, or step
Damn why can't I say that to him

When you're not loving me correctly
you're stepping on me, I'm no doormat
Can't cut you anymore slack
Show me you really want your woman back
We have love but we can't make it off just that
I'm sensitive sometimes, don't always trust me, like a thug
In need of your kisses and hugs,
while drowning in your actions of love
Affection mixed with imperfections

We are only human
I have more than a penny for your thoughts
I'd pay much more than a nickel for your kiss
I can promise you this

I'd wish upon billions of stars to be where you are
While cleaning your plate, I stay on your tastebuds
but I wanna be in your thoughts
Salivate over the being that is me
I can hear your heart beat
Does it still beat for me?
Are you still in awe of our chemistry?
I want you bad yet I can do bad by myself
Love me correctly and in the now
Dang, I forgot you just don't know how
My love language is foreign
I just wanna blow trees, sip Hennessy
and end up pleasing you on my knees
Guess I'm just too damn boring
My sex game stay having you snoring
Baby, I'd still wish upon a billion stars to be right where you are,
when you get your shit together
I'm ready for that forever

I choose you

In disbelief
Can't believe that my wingspan can withstand the storms
Although in between chaos
I appreciate the sun's kiss
The warmth I don't want to depart with
I remember when I was afraid to fly
You told me, "baby soar"
Believe in your wings
Don't worry no more

We have flown like a two man crew,ever since
Baby I can't forget about you
'Cause you're heaven sent
Do you know when you found me, I was looking for you too
Never chased a man it wasn't my style
But my soul attracted yours some how

My soul chose yours
The connection was electric
The bolts were insane
Placing beautiful love ballets on my brain
Along with a chorus in my heart
Baby they got a crush on you
But you don't feel the way they do
Although I thank his fans
I'm his biggest groupie
Don't shoot me
He can be your MCM
But respect that in reality it's me and him

We soared
He was so confident until we really started to take off
My love said *"I ain't never did this before,
the universe told me I could do it with you,*

Just take off with her that's all you need to do"
I love that man
He is my favorite dude
Glad we traded in the, I
For the
L
O
V
E
Cause I love me some
YOU
Keep flying with me

Push Start

Our men need healing too
When is it safe for a black man to cry
and express what he feels inside?
He needs a safe place to release
Why not in the arms of a black woman?

She is a nurturer of beings, the definition of peace
Call her Shine because her light beams
How may we help you?
Can we be of service?
Grant us a "Yes"
I know this isn't a simple request
Can I get it right with you?

I don't know how many of us there are on earth
but we have enough,
producing more by the day
because little black boys will become black men
that will need their "safe place."

Can we take a stand?
Or how about a vow, you don't think you can do it?
Baby I will show you how
You are my lifesavers and I am yours
Problems, we will face together
I'm your safe place and you are my shelter
We dwell in a house of real trust
Come what may, we must always communicate

I have to know when to listen,
you have to know when to talk
We both will reciprocate
We are a finely crafted machine yet we resemble art
You do the honors of pressing start

See, I couldn't be Rose on Titanic,
we both fitting on the piece of wood got damnit
It's something in me that wants to save you
deep down in your heart, you wanna save me too
Come to your safe place
I'm waiting on you

I Love You

If I could love you past your pain would you allow it?
Or would you work overtime to push me away?
During the process would you,
turn my blue skies grey?
I can only say I love you a million times
With my actions a million and two
But will that do?
See you need a healing and I'm offering that to you
Yep you need a healing and I might need one too
So don't fight the feeling
Scared, so you push away
Fearful, so you cheat,
now she ain't gonna stay
We don't even have to live this way
Those games don't have to be played
Struggling to love yourself, I get it
Navigating through uncharted waters can be a challenge
But you got a friend in me
You got a partner 'til the end in me
However, you must allow me to love you
In exchange you have to love me too
I can't beg you
Just unlock that door and say no more

Oh y'all got me writing lol

Chocolate Dreams

I had a dream about you
The room was pitch black,
yet you shined bright
Come invade my space as you plant kisses upon my face
I heard your heart beat and it matched mine
Your skin is a reflection of pure beauty
King you are a blue black cutie
I'm truly in awe
Huge fan of the black man
Black mixed with black I'm with all of that
Let's make black babies that will drive us both crazy
See I was just sitting here thinking about your scent
Can you leave it in every room you enter
and on both sets of my lips?
I wanna fall asleep so I can see you
Gazing upon you with my eyes closed will have to do
Taking trips to dreamland
hoping that one day you will land in my reality
Lavender on my pillow
Melatonin poppin
Butt ass naked sleep,
awaiting the man of my dreams

Home Run

Can I trade you an I for an US?
A couple forevers is a must
I remember when I couldn't trust
My heart was broken into pieces
by a lover I shared children with
My guard had been up since
You came in and had me caught in a world wind,
ready to throw the towel in

Shoot you changed me baby
Thought I was done now I want the ring and more babies
Be careful how you display me
I'm thinking social media won't see us
until the wedding photographer releases pictures
J.Wiggins behind the lens capturing our good features
No kidding my good side winning
I love the Most High
but when I first saw you, I thought about sinning
You restored my faith in the black man
I really was ready to give up, you just don't understand
I was about to be walking hand and hand with a chick,
soft on the eyes and small hands

Glad I stayed on course
With you the love wasn't forced
You don't even get mad when these previous half asses pop up
You laugh and say shit like *"I know why they still poppin' up"*
Tongue out, you stay clowning like what the fuck?

I love a funny man baby you got me stuck
Not the biggest guy but you ain't no punk
Intelligent and street smart baby that's a plus
I love you forever and always, you know what?
You call me strong but you rescued me

Your love was the cure for me
So I will raise you a forever for a few lifetimes
Cheesing ear to ear when yo' T Jones called me daughter
Glad she kisses you on your cheek
Moms don't know her son a freak
My mouth dry
but the lips below on sink
If you give me the wink,
fuck dessert we going home
With you I don't even fake moan
I knew you were special thank God I wasn't wrong

What About Love

Can love just be enough?
Even though I'm giving you so much more
I look forward to hello and never goodbye
You and I have a bond that can't be matched
Matter of fact I was made for you
In return the Most High made you for me
Even in the dark I hope you see me
I love your flaws and all
You don't have to be 6 foot tall
I'm in awe of you
Celebrating each moment with you
Your parents showed their asses when they made you
Love can keep anyone that wants to be kept
Put your hand in mine
I promise to protect you as you protect me
Two peas in one amazing pod
Ready to continue our forever
You have introduced me to a vibe that I can't live without
An energy I can't breathe without
When time runs out and we are old and grayish
I will repay the memories of us
All those years just aren't enough
Find me next life time
Forever mine

Visions Of You

Tossing and turning
I can remember your face
What you were wearing and even your taste
I had dreams of you
Long before we ever crossed paths
The dreams were so detailed, right down to your laugh
I fell in love with the essence of you
Your mere presence in my dreams wasn't enough for me
Baby you changed me
I sucked at love until you came along
A beautiful being of my very own
Sometimes I watch you sleep and think, how lucky I am
Then I shake my head and think how blessed I am
To be laying right next to you
I can't buy you all you want
However I can fulfill all your needs
I love you for loving me for me
You didn't handle me the way you did others
Your past didn't make me wonder
I'm a visionary
you were my muse before you ever amused me
The smell of your skin compels me
With your wide nostrils, inhale me
You are the only him I see
During those dreams I never wanted to wake up
Now I don't wanna go to sleep while you're up
God must have a sense of humor
The closer I get to you, the more we become one
I'm corny and you love it

Mr. Kinda Perfect

The Dream blurred in the background
as he kissed me deeply.
I was completely weak in the knees
SWV need to call Aidan and see about me.
How can this even be?
I really rolled the dice
and thought twice about even entertaining him.
My curve game was vicious with him.
Guess patience wrapped in consistency is what I needed.
My wall was higher than most.
You found the climb to be easier than most.
Ever since you took me by the hand
I truly understand how the love from such a man is special.
So precious and rare.
I love the scent of your hair and how your feet are always cold.
I love how you look at me and see my best.
Even in my worse times.
Your love is divine.
Glad you weren't a waste of my time.

Love That's Spoken

You are a manifestation of what my heart desired.
A living image of the very words I spoke.
The Most High sprinkled something extra on you.
Feeling like I'm truly at home around you.
Laying on the bed telling each other our dreams.
I bet you didn't know that I felt your energy in my dreams.
Sex isn't anything but a spiritual transition with you.
Guess that's how that rare love do.
Intimacy is real with you.
You had my mind before ever having my body.
That's the god in you.
Connecting with the god in me and it seems to be magical.
You restored my faith in men.
Reaffirmed my outlook on love.
Now I just wanna love you for life.
Day dreaming about being your wife.
We've already endured so much.
Yet never lost sight of us.

Black Storm Super Love

Ororo Munroe
As I grace the streets of Cairo
My mother a Kenyan tribal princess
Your kind would refer to mum as a witch.
Father not of the Bible but he's David,
representing Harlem, baby I can't shake it .
Storm I embraced it.
Gifted with the abilities to do things you mere human have never seen.
For me there are no limits.
I am a woman, a mutant, a thief, a X-Men,
a lover, a wife, a queen.
I am all these things.

I am Storm!
Being powerful sometimes can make you feel powerless.
I remember when I yearned for a love,
that was as black as the night.
He was a king and I vowed to be is wife.
The motherland called me home.
Africa held my heart and throne.

T'Challa
My heart skipped beats just by pronouncing your name.
Most don't know we had met before
It's crazy how the universe reopens doors.
We crossed paths during childhood.
After my parents were murdered I was up to no good.
Even superheroes have heartbreak.
Yet I fell in love with a Black Panther
while being my best storm.
In Wakanda our first and only child was born.
I gazed upon my black kings face
as I pushed our prince into the world.
In that moment we had not a care in the world.

No X-MEN
No Average
Just us and our people
However, the world is always under attack
and we have to SnapBack
Storm and Black Panther
We cherished the moments when mum and father
Are our only titles
What would life be like to just be king and Queen

T'Challa and Ororo
Our love was just as powerful as our powers
Superheroes yet lovers
setting up talking for hours
I posses this mighty power
but my weakness is my kings touch
Wakanda forever!

Black love come whatever
Pinch me if I'm dreaming
I want this love to last forever
We didn't get our Eternity
The most powerful mutants-him and me
But couldn't conquer the marriage thing
However our love lasted a lifetime
The pleasure was yours and mine

Lying In Church

I heard church bells ringing
before the choir start singing
You chose today to let your true colors show
Why today?
Bringing up old dates of your dealings
Got me feeling like I was just a sexual healing
You thought you could find healing between legs
Legs that weren't mocha thick
that spread to the heavens and most men call her heaven sent
Not just for her bedroom abilities,
for her ability to speak life into the almost dead

That spark in her that makes her wanna ride for you
without you telling her to
You just don't get it
While I was eliminating one stalker,
you were busy creating another
Shhhhhh, baby your mommy issues are showing

This problem you have, you already knew
Finally telling the truth wasn't for me
Suga that was for you
Even now, I'm praying that karma takes it easy on you
Although a small fraction of me wants you to feel the way that I do

I heard church bells ringing
In my head you were signing
Must have been dreaming
You selfish as hell
You wanna be Jada
I didn't get to be Will
This can't be how August feels
man you lied in July

Thought I was all out of tears
But like a bald head bitch, baby I cried
Because I don't understand hoe phases
or cheating
These are uncharted waters
with waves that produce bottom feeding
I could have handled the truth,
you could have saved that lie that multiplied,
now how do we divide this hurt?

They say don't date a poet
Don't fuck up and you wont get this work
But I heard church bells ringing
Bitches from yo' past
that were crying are now singing

My Mascara Is Ruined

He doesn't realize the hurt he inflicts
It's always this "try to turn it around" shit
I'm not your skeleton in the closet
I've been here so long and you still don't see me
Worthy of more than years of unprotected sex and great vibes
I remember when I thought I was the queen of our tribe
To think that I was there for you,
on one of the saddest days of your life
Yet I wasn't welcomed to one of the happiest
I had to ask the Most High
"What the fuck is wrong with me?"
Something has to be broken in me

If you ever left this world I wouldn't be able to take it
No matter how you told me you wanted to be back in your home town
not a body in a grave but as a huge tree
I'd have no right to state this request
Because I am invisible in your life outside of my walls
If I died tomorrow you wouldn't even ball
Likely wouldn't give my family a call
Your Facebook post if you even made one
Would probably read just my name and RIP
You wouldn't say that's my woman
and she meant the world to me
There would be no reference of the years we've been together
You say you don't know why you do the things you do
Let me stop you,
you do hurtful shit because you simply choose to
I made it to chapter four of the book of "kinda US"
Sick to my stomach wondering why did I have to go through so much
Why would loving you have to be so tough
Today you hurt me to my core
and I could only tell the truth and not fuss

"I love you" shouldn't mean nothing
to the women you treat like nothing
You can't understand the pain
unless some woman comes along and does all of this to you
But I wouldn't wish this hurt on even you

Mourning You

I had the most exciting news the other day
I immediately picked up my phone and dialed your number
Hung up instantly
I had forgotten that quickly that you are no longer with me
There were no "sorry for your loss texts"
No I didn't post *RIP My Love* on social media

How do I cope?
Falling to the floor
My breathing became shallow
Head hung the lowest of lows
No lust
Just love and trust
I prayed for you,
after the pain was inflicted I stayed with you
Remaining true
What did you do?
I can no longer physically touch you

I'm mourning someone that's still alive
No he didn't die
Perhaps the love did
Honestly, honesty and trust had been deceased
I wanted so much to believe he was the man he *"post"*to be
Or even the man he allows others to see
Outsiders stay calling him king
amongst other glorious words

The years weren't all bad
Our love story wasn't all sad
I thought one day he'd meet my dad
but that day won't ever come
Turning my back on him wasn't easy nor fun

Yet at this point it had to finally be done
I'm grieving, sick to my stomach
Going through the stages
Turning life's pages
and I just wanna have the good memories
He came to me in a dream the other night
'tho it gave me a fright
I was elated to have him in my sights
Dear Most High make it alright
Giving my all wasn't enough for him
Traveling miles to comfort him
gave no reassurance that I was definitely the one

Plans we made will now play out with others
Even now without closure I still wonder why?
Who wastes someone's years
Brings them pleasure but many tears
You confirmed my greatest fear
Not knowing if love, real love, will ever dwell here

I fought for you mentally
Physically I fought because of you
but in defense of myself
In the early stages of your departure,
felt like I had nothing left
I guess just knowing I really gave my all
Just to fall head over hills then flat on my ass
I'm repeating the past
You were supposed to protect me from this pain
I reckon I only have myself to blame
Mourning the loss of you all the same
No royal blue casket
No flowers or balloon release

I wasn't seated in the front pew
screaming for God to bring you back
He is alive and well as a matter of fact
But I am in mourning asking the Most High why
Learning coping skills to mask how I truly feel inside
What if I never trust again because of you

I deserve real love
even more now because of the bull you put me through
The history remains all the same
Avoided accompanying the same space as you
I have this great distaste for you
Cheers to another day of mourning you

Dedication With Exclamation

I dedicate this poem to heartbreak
To the men that entered my life
pretending to be something that they just weren't
I love you, merely words with no actions
To the man that thought while living his life in the fast lane,
I'd be a distraction
Yeah I dedicate this poem to
the man that strung my along for years
Being my knight in shining armor one day only to be the monster in my
bed the next
Thinking how can I be so madly in love with this caliber of man
The outside world couldn't ever understand
He is mister almost prefect to everyone
Because they never have been in love with him
Never endured his voice saying "I love you" only to then not call for days
I bet they have never laid naked in the bed with him
As he traces your body with his tongue
and plants his lips on every opening
This poem is dedicated to the man that told me his secrets
and made me feel safe enough to tell him mine
I swear I didn't tell you my fears so that you could become them
Heartbreak was something I understood more than love
Baffled how you literally treated our relationship like a job
Doing just enough all these years to not get fired
Sweetheart I dedicate this poem to you
After all the hell you put me through and others to
I still yearn to have a man with walnut skin like you
Defined as black in America
I still desire a baritone voice with dark eyes
Still betting on black like my gut tells me to
Even tho I crapped out betting on a few
I dedicate this poem to the wound that finally healed
Still desiring to know how real love feels

Forever Wounds

Be at peace with the pieces of me that you misused
This stinking sore,
can't ever seem to be a healing wound
You look at me and my heart skips a beat
However that same heart you trampled under your feet
With you I accept defeat
No energy left to fight
Two wrongs don't make it right but honestly,
I don't have the mindset to do the things you did to me

We all have the ability to be toxic
yet I just don't have the will to be
Only wanted beauty and positivity pouring from me
See I just wanted to cook you meals
Be the one to fill you up and be in absolute awe of you
Building you a home filled with peace and tranquility
My years were already planned with you in mind
Memories of holidays
and vacations popping up on our timelines

Outside taking in Summer's breeze
while you and I swing
Cigars and good whiskey,
more than my man your a friend to me
I foreseen us outside on the porch
watching our grandchildren play
Some how all those plans will forever be delayed
Why are you so fearful of loving me?

I have tried for years to navigate your mind
to discover the mysteries of your heart
You don't have to keep leaving me in the dark
I remember your darkest time I was there

Don't know if you were surprised I'd came that far
Baby if your hurting then I'm hurting,
I need to be where you are
This sore is oozing,
no amount of first aid nor bandaids can help
Please stop picking at my wounds and battle scars
The aid you can give is changed behavior
No more sorry or mind games
The hurt you inflect claim it and change it
I was just setting here thanking about how you changed me
How your misusage of "I love You" really rearranged me

Love Countdown

You had 24 hours
and I couldn't even get a few minutes of your time
Guess love is blind and you failed at time management
I will not be your *"Quarantine"* booty
Your, *"it's almost the end of the world cutie"*
Your *"bounce back because you know where my heart is at"*
The clock is ticking
I'm hoping and wishing that you have finally come to your senses
I wanted badly to be the one
and you so badly want to run me off
Loving me correctly shouldn't be a coin toss
I can't go back won't go back
to how hurtful this love use to be
Nobody saved me but me

I heard cheers the day I threw in the towel
Friends were going wild
Yes, it took awhile for me to start to heal
Felt as if my heart was outside of my chest, wounded
yet still beating slowly
The only thing that could repair this damage was detoxing from you
My knight in shining armor
Had become the monster under my covers, rocking my bed
In my head I had processed the truth
Took longer for my heart to receive the data
and get on board about the matter
Months passed and I felt better

Not having to think about if I'm the only one
No day dreaming about birthdays you missed
or our very last kiss
You popped back up
something in my gut told me to keep not responding

Yet something in your words sounded so peaceful and calming
I was missing my friend
Attached to my favorite body and beautiful grin
But you had 24 hours today
the clock has rundown
You had 24 hours
to love me in the now
Damn you still don't know how

Somebody's Son

Where a beautiful flower once bloomed in rich soil
He single handedly pulled me up from my roots,
planted seeds of insecurities and doubts
I'm not one to pout
Although, for months
I have still been administering this benefit of doubt
You changed me
Years of your intentional disloyalty
and betrayal has brought me rainy days and hell
Trying to convince myself, all is well

My Coco complected cheeks are mo'wetter than dry
Eyes swollen from the cries
You can't even tell me why
Why would you inflict such pain on me
You will forever be the reason I won't trust
You will forever be the reason that my actions won't fuel effort
Fuck an apology,
a real sorry is changed behavior
You've never done me a favor so please do this
Don't allow your son to treat a woman he "loves " like this
I hope your daughter never bares witness to this
You crushed me for fun
I don't get it
If you wanted to continue to be a womanizing hoe
what did you bother me fo'?

I have never endured pain being single
The gut punches and wounds came after the mingle
Title of my sitcom "Happy Black and Single"
Sir you came and canceled my show
Took my shit off air
Turned it into a love story turned horror film
You are the monster in my bed

The self hate in my head
I don't want your pretending ass in my face,
occupying good space
If a heart is a house for love you demolished mine
Blasting you on social media won't give me satisfaction
A caption that reads *"he spreads STI's"*
will not heal this big hole I have inside

I remember you cried
I drove miles to wipe your tears
In pain I eased all of your mistakes
But got damnit you just take and take
In the looks department your alright
Talent department you're out of sight
Yet when it comes to love and honesty,
you just can't get right

I was a kept secret on my own terms
Never thought I'd be the women you'd burn
Yeah you changed me lesson learned
You're worse than my first perm, giving third degree burns
Spontaneously combust!
Erasing you from my mind & heart is a must
Your physical presence use to give me butterflies,
now just nausea
I'm trying to figure out what type of pain I ever caused ya

Unfortunately, all I did was love you
and be your full time fool
Allowing you break my love rules
I should get my brother to beat yo' little ass
I kid, my mentality don't work like that
Just give me my heart and years back
My pain has a name and face,
he's apart of the Superior race

Baby You Need A New Tire

I shall never cry again
from the pain a lover has caused
See I thought I knew him
but do we ever really know people?
He was my somebody when I wasn't looking for anybody
before we exchanged warm bodies
This black man let me in
Said he wasn't looking for a women
just to exchange bodily fluids with
That he was looking for his good thang and that I was it

He was tried of chasing tail
and pussyfooting with these lesser chicks
I told him my fears, expressed why I didn't want him near
because he is the type of black man I fear
The ones that pretend to have it all together
but their eyes tell a different story
Keep them peepers off of me
I don't wanna give you the glory
A black man like you knows exactly what to do
You wear this shell so well that I can't break through
Your pretend game was insane
Man kudos to you

Calling me your last name
but knowing that I wouldn't be your last
Accountability!
Yes, I allowed it to last
I went to my male friend,
Yea the one that says "He don't really fuck with me"
Dude keeps it's super real,
he gonna kick that real shit to me
He said, *"you wanna be married, married you will be"*
but you have drop that bald tire

and get a new wheel my Queen

Lost for words like "You don't know how I feel"
I was on some love shit
and bruh was just keeping it real
Truth hurts
I said truth hurts
He don't know how I feel
Thought this man was my forever
yet he is a bald tire and I need a new wheel
Shawty hurt me to the core
Now I'm keeping it real
I truly know now how heartbreak feels

Did I Manifest You

I prayed for you
so forgive me if I don't give up on you as fast as others do
Oh you gonna have to see me
Beyoncé pass the lemonade
Not jealous nor crazy
Shit, yo love got lazy
You hurt me
I'm wounded
Your hands are bloody
You've provided it
Now what's love got to do with it?
You ravaged my emotions and raped my heart
At the starting line you did a false start
Whats done in the dark
Just might not see light at the right time
It's never the right time to hold you accountable
But you do you
While I borrow somebody's hoe-handbook
Can I now be the crook
The taker and faker
I wanna know how real love feels
but forgive me if now I just want to be an empty vessel
Can I be the one but have many?
Activated my inner Lori Harvey
Serial dating maybe even allowing some penetration
Hold the love making
This ain't no love in the making
I'm just taking
Giving only got me got
So forgive me for my fake moans
Sorry my Sheba got extra wet for you
She doesn't know how to deactivate
Try to forgive the times I complained about never getting quality time
Please forgive me for being your rock

Only for you to treat me like
dirty feet on clean pillow cases
This is straight no chaser
I don't have exes
I have distant memories
But forgive me
You're a new level, a suppressed memory

Playback

He playing me like I'm not a greatest hit
Like I'm a song he plays at home
But never in his whip
These are my confessions
Thought he was a blessing but lately
I feel like Brandy going back and forth with Monica
The boy is mine but I'm sharing him with the streets
and all things in between
Even tho I'm feeling neglected,
in need of TLC, I won't creep
I need to be your pull up song
I need to be that track that brings you back to the good old days
That melody from heaven
that has your emotions open like seven eleven
As you rain down on me
My initials are SRW not SWV
Born in '87 but I'm that 90s R&B
that makes you wanna call your reverend
Because this music makes you sin
Baby making having twins
Then again you'll be ready to give me the sun stars and moon
Yet I just wanna be your favorite tune
Inconsistency isn't sexy
Putting your woman last and never first isn't cool
I'm feeling really foolish that I still wait up at night
Hoping to be trapped in your sight
To see the flash of your headlights
But that doesn't happen enough
I just want to be your favorite track
The one you play back
But his playlist is full
and I'm not made to be the track he skips
Just delete me from your playlist
Because I'm somebody's greatest hit

Blood Stained Love Letters

It might be always beyond my comprehension
how someone can hurt you to your core
Wound you in such a matter and still keep smiling
With lying eyes and a treacherous tongue
If breaking hearts was a sport that negro has overly won
I'm a trophy on his shelf collecting dust now
A physical reminder that love won't always love you back
I don't have many regrets in life
Yet I regret allowing a vassal so damaged into my life
Love must of really been hate
You don't treat someone you love in such a way
Hell I welcomed your sorry's
Masking the fact that you're just sorry
What an elaborate disguise
I don't even see you the same
Use to see an halo
Now I see horns
Pupils that use resemble gate ways to heaven
Now look like dark pits of hell
I could scream and yell I hate you
Gave you my heart
You crushed it with your small shoe
How mighty was the one that hurt you?
Or just maybe this is just you
The Victimizer who has never been the victim
Inflicting harm you never had to heal from
Painting this picture of being the pick of the litter
Funky dog head bitch,
you are now a permanent stitch
on a wound that will take me years to heal
I use to fight for you but now I have no will
Since an even exchange can't be called a robbery
You may never feel like I feel

POF

Oh there's plenty of fish in the sea
Bitch you didn't throw back a fish
You threw back a mermaid something rare

When she didn't bite your bait you switched it up
You came for her with a fishing reel made of steel
Not that Walmart special you usually use
Using a higher grad of bait for this here mate
Your regular old worm wouldn't do you had the prize
Yet you rather keep tossing out your line to catch guppies
Still haven't mastered it's quality over quantity
Congratulations, smart ass dummy
See you're the type that will chase a dollar bill
when you have a $100 in your wallet,
during the process get pick pocketed
It's plenty of fish
But every fish ain't me
I'm getting sick of these pretend kings
stringing good women along
Dude you know you ain't yet shit!
Leave that woman alone
She didn't shoot her shot,
You did the shooting
Not sure what game you're playing
but it doesn't take years
You are a good woman's worse fear
Oh she trippin? Because of you she looks at love different
Gave her heart to you because you claim to be different
I don't wanna here *"you chose him"*
Shit people switch up
He didn't pull off his mask I guess that bitch was stuck
At some point in life, I thought we all grow up
Trust and believe she ain't a nut
That man done wasted her years

Now trying to front
Was she just some butt,
when you were confusing your feelings and such?
I didn't get the memo
I love black men
but lesser beings I can't stand
Day one you know if you wanna be kept
They say we don't like the truth
Hell I will take it any day over a lie
There's no reason for you to kiss the girls and make them cry
I'm as curious as George so I'm asking why?
You scared of commitment
leave me be I'm not with it
You don't have time cool I won't even cross the line
You wanna be a loose dick trick?
Up front you let me know
I'm a 30 plus year old woman so I'm walking out the doe'
Keep it real so I won't be blinded
Throw me immediately back into the ocean I will do just fine
I will never again even tug at your line
There's only a few mermaids amongst the fish
I will be caught and kept in no time
But you're right it's plenty of fish in the sea
So you'll be fine

My Eyes Are Sweating

I cried the other day
Felt like the walls were caving in
and my strength alone couldn't hold them up
I cried last night because for the life of me
I couldn't understand how you could live your best life
while I was hurting
I needed you and you jetted
I have never felt so neglected
I just for once needed your physical presence
But the club was a priority
Events come first
I gave you my best but I got your worst
Man this shit hurts!
I just knew with all we've been through I could make us last
But this feeling won't pass
I've been there for you even when you wouldn't allow me to
Car, plane, or train I'm gonna get to you
Even if my feet will have to do
But where are you?
One phone call maybe a text
There is a difference from having love for someone
and being in love
You have shown me the difference over the years
while confirming my fears
I'm in love, I care too much
I pray for you so much but
You just care a little about me
You're not in love
Your actions reveal all things
So when clubs come first, friends too
A million and two other things come before me too
My blinders are off, I see
I was head over hills in love with someone

that only had a little love for me
Now I have to heal and prepare for something real
Deserving of more than being a long term pussy supply,
someone that will feed your soul and dry your eyes
But in the dark alone she cries
Just this one time I needed that same love baby
that I give to you
Guess this wasn't enough for you to come through

Quotable

He cut me so deep
I mean to the white meat
And he just watched me bleed
See the outside world thinks he is so grand
Females wishing they were in his bed
Praying to be the one rubbing his head
But these yamps don't know
The heartache of being in love with a professional hoe!
This isn't how love suppose to go

Missed Calls

Booms!
And thunder claps
A storm is underway and I'm worried about where you are
Calls and texts unanswered
But Facebook pictures liked
Now wondering if you even thought, about me and mine tonight
Yea, we are alright
I'm clearly not your candy rain
Because once again you left me out in the rain
and no I won't just hang dry
You brought tears tonight to my eyes
You just don't love the way I do
I try not to hold it against you
But damn
I wish just one time I'd be first and not last on your mind
I want to be unforgettable
Yet I'm so easily forgotten
Good enough to bone
Although not good enough for you to pick up the phone
Where did I go wrong?
Bleeding out but you won't apply pressure to my wound
If this is love then I'm doomed
I can't be the one you love it saddens me
because you just don't get the simple shit
So I quit!
Gone get
You won't turn me into a crazy bitch!
If my ass was on fire you wouldn't even grace me with your spit
I quit

I'm a victim of this one way love shit

Closed for Repair

I got so comfortable with being you're everything
that I lost me
Give me my heart back
Broken under construction,
I don't care just leave it there!
I loved with no strings attached
Gave you praise and pats on the back
All the while you were stabbing me in my back
Let's speaks facts
All I want is my bruised heart back
You wounded me and I need repair
What hurts most when you were damaged
I was there, your repair woman
Tool belt in hand ready to work
I love you so much it hurts
Just get out my face!
Leave me in my space!
But leave my heart before you leave my place

Cat Lady In The Making

She doesn't desire to be adored by many just one
He has mastered all things on his path
to being great all except one
loving her
See she wants a love she can feel
A body she can touch
More than a part time love
Or a here and there fuck
How amazing it must feel
When you love somebody that loves you too
He knows actually what to do
Your body's are like one huge wave crashing against the shore
Is it wrong to want to feel wanted by you?
Should I not long for your touch
Since you seem perfectly fine without mine
I can't wrap my mind around the fact we are just existing
When we should be living
Playing in the covers every night
Making love until we both climax, right
Our love making reaching new heights
But you must have a fear of high places
So you're afraid of cloud nine?
No it's not fine
We are stuck at start
So can you release my heart
Just loosen your grasp
I'm lonely with you
So what am I without you?
You are afraid of heights
That's why we are still on the ground

Return My Heart

I made the decision today that I want my heart back
Leave it at the door broken and wounded
I will take on the task or repairing it myself again
Exit left please
You are a pro at being ghost
When I need you the most, your never there
Your bailout game is on the highest level
My heart can't take any more pain,
so it's petal to the metal
You want love that you are to damn selfish to give back
You want loyal that you don't possess
Do you even realize that?
I damn near fully lost me behind you
Pushing dreams to the side that's, *Artistry Suicide*
So damnit leave my heart
I said leave my heart
Don't you dare take it with you y'all have to part
I rather bleed out on the MIC
Allow the claps snaps and screams to heal me
My very words to stitch me up

Selfish

Have you ever tried to give CPR
or first aid to yourself
Giving your all to someone that's selfish
because you're so selfless,
feels like that giving the shirt off your back
but yet never receiving one
I'm so cold
I wonder who gives to the giver?
Who's your lifeline when your the lifeline
The giver needs love too,
can I get a refill before you drain me dry damn you!
(But you so fucking selfish)
You selfish some of a bitch
Your love is like a test
and when I feel like I mastered it I still have to cram
I'm super freaky, heller geeky and got yams!
My heart is as big as my smile
I have given you so much
No take backs
I have driven miles and wouldn't take that back
I wiped yo' tears and always had your back
But you're so fucking selfish

You so got damn selfish
that you allowed me to love yo' damaged ass
Telling me you know you always fucking up
like those words give you a pass and such
I can't keep giving you the shirt off my back,
only to be left shirtless because you
will never give me one back

Giving energy and love to empty vessels that will never be filled up
Because my best is never enough for these types

That parasite type of mindset, I encounter it too often
Selfish people praying on selfless people
I don't have anything else to give to these damaged people that really
prefer to be broken
Gate keeper I have no more tokens
I have given so many away
Afraid of losing people
that have done everything in their power to loss me

Gate Keeper!
If you let me pass this one time
I will let go the rope and stop being these people's lifeline
Sounds good but might be lying
something in me makes me think I can fix people like him

That I can love a being past their pain
and in return they will do the same
Although that has never happened
Please pass me a napkin
Wet faces and stained pillow cases in most cases never to be seen
I need to turn my back and not ever look back
life cut me some slack
I have removed my cape

I have rescued so many, now I have to rescue me
Giving CPR and first aid to myself, because all I have is self
If I keep on giving without ever receiving,
I won't have anything left
I use to be afraid to ask the Most High
to remove people from my life that didn't give me the love and respect
I was giving them
Due to deep down I already knew the people that would be removed
Giving energy and love to empty vessels that will never be filled up
I wanna post yo' selfish ass picture up!
Yet I won't because you taught me
a man will only do what you allow him to do
If I was the woman for you that selfish shit wouldn't exist
I wanna call your granny but she doesn't know she raised a selfish bitch
You are a bad addiction that I'm cold turkey about to quit
Why do selfless people fall in love these selfish little shits?

Careless With Our Love

I woke up head pounding
Tears running down my face
My heart was beating so fast
you'd think I'd just finished a race
I had a dream about you
Yet I can't decipher if it was a sweet dream or a nightmare
In this dream I was the complete opposite of myself in reality
I was totally transparent
Heart on my sleeve
Begging you to stay and we continue this
whatever this is
You gave the same excuses you do in life
But instead of just not giving two shits, I gave a few
I don't even think you realize the hell I've been through
After I realized I was awake and laying right next to you
I got a pain in my heart
I held my chest as you rolled over
and caressed my leg
I wish I could interpret dreams
So I could know what this all means
Because I'm battling loneliness in real life
If I feel by myself then why I'm I laying next to you?
I'm in a beautiful nightmare
involving me and you
Where feelings are expressed
But we are still at start
Been through so much yet still at halt
, this is truly my fault
I knew I was ready for something bigger,
you stated you were too
but your actions never reflected your words that was the proof
When your actions and words didn't match up
I should have packed up

But I didn't
Having a fraction of you was better than having none of you at all
So I thought

Damn I wish you were the man you pretend to be

Give & Receive

Don't ask me to do shit for you that you won't do for me
If you won't drive in a storm for me
Guess what?
Don't ask me to get wet for yo' ass either
See I figured it out
You can give a man the stars
and he will ask why you didn't bring the entire universe
Damn you never satisfied
It's not enough to treat you like gold fallin' out your ass huh?
When we both know,
you don't do half of the shit I do for you
So forgive me if I got to leave you where you stand
I don't wanna be feeling lonely
When I'm supposed to have a man
It's not hard to understand
Don't ask me to do shit that you won't do for me
You don't cook me meals and buy me things
Wash my clothes or my back
Then don't ask me for shit like that
I truly believe that every man we encounter
Aren't worthy of the love we bring
My love is heavy
Like a pimp with a limp
I'm too cool to even trip
So I will send you on your way
Because you're not ready to be treated the way I treat a man
Nah little daddy you still don't understand
It's not all about you
Nor what a woman can do for you
Real men do shit too
So if your 'taker' ass still haven't got a clue
Don't ask me to do shit
That you want do for me too

Eyes Wide Open

Ever since I removed my blinders
shit just hasn't been the same
Just another name in your phone
A text message remaining on delivered
I wish real love would come back in style
Can consistency be a new hot trend
I was born in the wrong era
Long dresses cooking good foods in the kitchen
Got the children settled and washed up
awaiting your arrival for dinner
Daddy gets the big piece of chicken
Love making finger licking because it's actually love
Afterwards we set on the porch surrounded by the night sky
I'm at peace with my peace next to me
My love and loyalty isn't set up for this time
Crank up the time machine and send me back in time
So I may encounter a love like mine

Underneath The Dark Moon

It's dark
I can't even see my hand in front of my face
Confused as to why you'd treat me this way
The last time I walked out, you didn't follow
Why was I surprised that you didn't even blink this time?
As water hits my cheeks
Throat too tight to speak
I believed in us
Never wanted to fuss
My best years were invested in us
Now I'm questioning trust
Was it love or just lust?
No in God we trust
The palm of your hand met my face
My heart went from a steady beat to a race
Love don't live here anymore just fear
I don't have anymore tears
Just need to get out of here
No wedding cake toppers for us
Flowers that once bloomed are now wilted
My hunger for love you killed it
Will power to go on is gone
Walking on this cold night with my hands shaking
holding my purse tight
He could of easily killed me this time
Guess this is the down side of love
Punches and slaps vs kisses and hugs
I don't know where I'm going
Haven't seen my folks in months
Brother said don't come back with that punk
Love is blind and my 20/20 vision was definitely shot
Daddy tried to come get me months ago
I told him "daddy fucking go home"

I was dead wrong
Home is no longer home
he forced me to change my phone number
Removed all contacts
His forceful hand I was under
Broken ribs and cries in the dark
Fired from my job
I could no longer call in to take time to heal black eyes
Trapped in this nightmare, I just wanted to die
Understanding why people submit to suicide
Most High protect me this night
Yes I was wrong but don't neglect me
The moon doesn't look right much darker tonight

Why Her?

I remember it like it was yesterday.
Me passing you in the hallway .
Minding my own business headed to the cafe
When you said, *"Sharita right?"*
I would have never thought that would turn into an invite.

2015 and I hadn't missed a birth since
Until Covid-19 hit
Yet it wasn't because of social distancing
Guess I was put on the bench
But it was never spoken.
When I took that forced break and you came back, I was hoping.
That you finally realized you had the golden token.
I was so focused on trying to understand why the change.
I allowed your trauma to over look you inflicting pain
I won't claim to know the heartache this passed year brought you.

Although I know it should of taught you to love better and to be better
Being a good human would have helped you sleep better.
I don't remember her being around
when your crown was knocked down.
So why her?
During our jam session,
blowing smoke clouds to backseat your stressing.
We talked 'US'
in reality it was really her and us
So why her ?
She wasn't brought to light into an opening night.
I knew something wasn't right
You assured me that it wasn't what it seemed
I was still your coffee and you were my sugar and cream.

Baby trust me, you said trust me.
So how the hell is she calling you subliminally her king?

Oh we've been friends forever.
I introduced her to her now ex husband and whatever.
Come to think of it that was kinda clever .
She knows about us but she has a thing for me
So business just isn't business.
Who teams up with a female with feelings, you must be kidding

New message :
I know a lots been going on come have drinks with me

Clearly I didn't drink enough.
I asked you straight up were you fucking with her
You said hell no
then processed to throw her and her customer service under the bus
Looked me in the face going on about such and such
My spirt was bothered.

Leaving and you even asked me to stay
Everything in me said yo' ass was lying that day.
Within less than two days your entire story changed
You slept with others including her,
but it was out of convience
How fucking convenient?
Honestly being honest just isn't your truth
You lie so much only you should believe you.
Why her ?
Because she outed you to social media?
Or because she was already claiming you and didn't need your approval?
It's a lot of bitch in your pedigree I now see
Because if in all those years I was honest
You could of been honest with me.
But I'm the one you love and you'd never hurt me
It all comes out in the wash and bitch you dirty
How you get him is how you lose em
so sis the karma will be rather worthy
So why her?

Oscar Worthy

When I think of you
I think about stepping in dog shit and it ruining my new shoes.
I did not sign up to be a part of your rendition of sister wives.
The OKC black edition.
I rebuke you, lying ass negro I have to mute you.
See we are who we choose to be.
Everybody wasn't lying on you.
The only one lying was in fact you.
Disgrace to any person that has ever called you king.
Compared you to any godly things
because you are far from your higher self.
Damn you must not even love yourself.
In denial about the hurt you inflect,
afraid to except the consequence.
This is no coincidence.
You hid your true self for reason.
I should publicly behead you with my sharp ass words,
you foul ass turd.
Although you've already hung yourself
With your thick rope of lies
You didn't get a top shelf prize
Just another broken vessel with a vagina
that actually welcomes your deceit
Eat your cake of betrayal without a spoon
Allow your foul moves to be your tomb
I never casted you in videos
because for years you've been acting
The role of a dog you need no practice
Damn I stepped in some shit today, it remained me of you
Got damn I was wearing my favorite shoes

Our Souls Connect

Our connection was a blessin'
Trust me I'm not flexin.
You were suppose to be my last.
Last French kiss, Last love
Last man to ever explore my insides
Now I'm playing back our good times
but the bad times keep entering my mind.
Was I not enough?
I'm trying to suck this hurt and pain up
Really confused, thought it was me and you.
Emotions make you cry sometimes.
I'm all cried out.
You took my heart stepped on that shit then you bounced.
I'm not ready to announce we are over,
no PSA was made when we began.
I didn't just lose my mans,
I lost my friend.
The person that I was excited to tell good news to.
The man that I would so quickly protect.
You know the one you nourish and never neglect?
Wish I could say we aren't finished yet.
But my mind says we're done.
My heart says, not yet.
My soul isn't ready to disconnect.
What the heck!
You only cheated,
You only lied,
You only confirmed my fears.
You were only the reason I revisited that dark place inside
Too strong of a person to lose my mind
Although I wanted to show you my hands and feet
Stomp you out then repeat,
Maybe you and the fat end of my bat need to meet.

I can speak it but not follow through
Mad as hell
Negro you know I really love you
No -ed at the end of love because it's not past tense
Was the connection not enough?
Was the chemistry too much?
Did my craving for your touch
and wanting to make so much love become tough?
Were they worth it?
I have so many questions.
Like 21 questions well really more like 50.
I've convinced myself that you never loved me
Hard pill to swallow because how could that be
Too many years and the energy doesn't lie
A complete puzzle that's now missing a center piece.
Give my heart back at least
I'm not ready to disconnect.
Have we finished yet?

You Aint Shit
"The Kickback"

If he doesn't use brushes or combs
don't bring that bald trick home or whatever the Bible says.

You have activated my inner bitch.
I know you've been dying to call me this
Truth be told some men ain't shit
Thanks for proving it
You're flea bitten wolves in men's clothing.
Apart of an unworthy pack
I stepped in some shit the other day, it reminded me of you.
Do you prefer being called Kaka or pooh?
I'm tried of you foul fools.
We are the earths treasure not rusty tools.
See a woman can have her shit together,
be pretty in the face, thick in waist and High IQ .
Yet she still ends up being played by a punk like you.
Good gentlemen's this isn't for you.
A drunk soul doesn't lie.
You a *Harvey Weinstein* type of guy.
Get yo damn peepers off me, raw dawgin'
probably spreading STDs.
Please don't even sneeze
Man you a fuckin' sleaze
Thinking it's cute yelling creep squad!
Okay Richie D .
I hope you grabbed his car keys 'cause
Your boy Pissy drunk
and I EAT 'ain't shit' dudes like him for lunch.
Fuck it, bon appétit we can have brunch.
But you prefer dinner, rooms with dime light.
Tonight you can be the victim.
Ain't no damn 12 play
Boy you can play but watch who you play with,

84

that's all I'm gonna say.
But when you see a real king send him my way
You ain't shit
Stubby dick
You ain't shit
But a trick
Hopefully your seed doesn't participate in creating a daughter one day.
You think you get a pass for treating women any old kinda way
Karma doesn't care about your juvenile mind set, or fucked up ways,
nor why you still don't get it yet
It's coming to collect.

Featured in the "Poetic City" Short film, "The Kickback"

Mouth From the South
Belle Publishing

What Lies in Truth
Tameika Mishay

Let Me Spit:
Love & Hate
Bennie Books

The Mix: Evolu...
Orgasms & Dinner Dates
Sharita Renee

Bennie's Books
Bennie Publications

We help Indie artists edit, self-publish, promote,
and market their literature.

Are you a business owner?
We teach self-publishing, for those who desire to help
others self-publish as well.

Contact us for more information
Owner: Joelisha Fairbanks   918-873-0250
Co-Owner: Tre'Auntae Fairbanks   405-800-6017

Email: BenniePublications@gmail.com

"Change the world, one book at a time."

Acknowledgments

There are so many individuals to acknowledge On this journey to book three. It has been emotional, yet beautiful. A huge piece of my healing process are on these very pages.

Thank you to my children, whom have showed me that unconditional love is just that. Kyla, Donatella, and Cerventes, you are my treasure, the golden pot at the end of rainbows. Y'all are my legacy. Love each one of you beyond any words I could ever write.

Bennie Publications, oh we got that three-peat! This ride with you has been amazing. Joelisha Fairbanks, nothing but love and light queen. Thank you for handling my art with such care.

Lewie P / MarLee Lewis thank you for your art, your time, and your
energy. From book two to book three. You blessed my book covers and also me.
Your art gives people so much peace, laughter and utter joy.
Salute to you king.

To family and friends that prayed for me during this process. The healing that continues and the effects of 2020. I love you and thank you so much. I didn't slow down this year. I truly sped up. If you poured into me even a drop, I thank you.

Lastly I'd like to thank the love that I've healed from. Where there's heartbreak there is also growth. Your test blind sided me but my testimony baby it's one for the ages. You seen the evolution of my pen and pad. Now you will view my transition to new heights from the sideline. Where there isn't forgiveness there is acceptance and best wishes.

Thank you and all praises to the Most High.

About The Author

Sharita Renee Wilson. Author of The Mix: Evolution Of The Pen and Pad & *Orgasms & Dinner Dates*. Vice President of *Poetic City*, Spoken word artist, writer and Entrepreneur amongst other titles. Jones born and Spencer raised she uses her platform to empower her community. Passionate about Mental health and the youth. This mother of three is an activist for true freedom and unity, through her words she hopes to teach self love and healing. Her poetry is a product of her life and others. Stage name Sharita Renee because she has always believed in the strength of her own name. No matter the genre she paints a beautiful picture with her words.

ISBN: 978-1-7354367-1-5

Any references to historical events, real people, or real places are used fictitiously.
Names, characters, and places are products of the author's imagination.

Front cover image by Marlee *"Lewie P" Lewis*

Printed in the United States of America.
First printing edition November 2020.

www.ingramcontent.com/pod-product-compliance
Lightning Source LLC
Chambersburg PA
CBHW041413010726
47507CB00005B/262